Our House

by Theresa Rebeck

A SAMUEL FRENCH

SAMUEL FRENCH

FOUNDED 1830

NEW YORK HOLLYWOOD LONDON TORONTO

SAMUELFRENCH.COM

ISBN 978-0-573-69880-4   Printed in U.S.A.   #29647

MUSIC USE NOTE

IMPORTANT BILLING AND CREDIT REQUIREMENTS

OUR HOUSE was produced by Playwrights Horizons (Tim Sanford, artistic director; Leslie Marcus, managing director; Carol Fishman, general manager) in New York City in June 2009. The performance was directed by Michael Mayer, with sets by Derek McLane, costumes by Susan Hilferty, lighting by Kenneth Posner, and sound by Darron L. West. The production manager was Christopher Boll and the production stage manager was James FitzSimmons. The cast was as follows:

JENNIFER	Morena Baccarin
ALICE	Katie Kreisler
STU	Stephen Kunken
GRIGSBY	Mandy Siegfried
MERV	Jeremy Strong
VINCE	Haynes Thigpen
WES	Christopher Even Welch

CHARACTERS

WES

JENNIFER

STU

ALICE

MERV

VINCE

GRIGSBY

(The door opens. **WES** *and* **JENNIFER** *enter, talking with professional enthusiasm, overlapping.)*

WES. I am so glad that you could make time, it's really –

JENNIFER. No, please, it's a great honor, my god –

WES. Because I know you must be slammed right now –

JENNIFER. No more so than you –

WES. 'Cause you're getting a lot of attention, at the network level we are well aware of what's happening for you –

JENNIFER. I've been very fortunate lately, but that's –

WES. Fortunate, are you kidding? Everybody's talking. What a string of, the thing on Beirut, that incredible interview with Mel Gibson –

JENNIFER. *(overlap)* I have a terrific producer.

WES. *(continuing)* Unbelievable what you got him to, and then that piece you did on Darfur? Phenomenal.

JENNIFER. *(overlap)* Like I said, my producer is excellent.

WES. *(overlap)* No no, come on, not the producer, don't be modest. I hate modesty, I don't know why anyone thinks its a virtue because it's not.

JENNIFER. Oh –

WES. I hate it.

JENNIFER. Oh, I'm not –

WES. Am I wrong about this? I could be wrong. But that piece, what you did. Those women? I had tears. And I don't cry. I mean, right? I do not cry. Tears running down my face.

(reaching for her jacket)

Come on, let me take, relax, relax. Make yourself comfortable. A glass of wine, can I get you

JENNIFER. A glass of white would be –

WES. *(off her jacket)* Wow, this is lovely. What is this, Prada –

7

JENNIFER. Dolce.

WES. Very nice. How much am I paying you? Don't answer that.

(He hangs it up; goes to get the wine, opens it.)

So. Your star is on the rise. This is not news to you, or to anyone, obviously.

JENNIFER. Well –

WES. What I just said is the simple truth, Jennifer; you wouldn't be here, with me, if it weren't. Well, you might because you're an absurdly attractive woman and it's just possible that I would ask for a meeting just for an excuse to spend the night flirting with you but that's a different matter. Did I say that? Is that harassment? Please tell me that's not harassment. Please tell me I'm still allowed to tell a beautiful woman that she's beautiful. I don't want to live in a world where that's not an acceptable thing to say.

JENNIFER. There's no one here but me, so I think you're safe.

WES. Very politic. I like that!

(He hands her a glass.)

JENNIFER. Thanks.

WES. *(off wine)* Oh, that is good. I'm just starting to appreciate the whites. My wife had one of those courses come to our house, have you ever done that? Where they bring the whole, fifteen different wine glasses at every place setting and the guy tells you what it all means? Phenomenal. Fucking annoying as hell because you can't leave, if the guy turns out to be a moron, you can't just take off because he's in your fucking house, but that's beside the point. This guy was pretty good, taught me a few things. The whites, he taught me the screw cap is a good thing.

(smelling) What is that, pear, some floral, maybe some crushed stone –

JENNIFER. Crushed stone?

WES. You can't taste the crushed stone in there? Maybe it's just me, I have a penchant for scorched earth or something. Jennifer Ramirez, you are a phenomenal reporter. What they've had you doing in New York, our affiliate, we are duly proud, I think, of our record, Edward R. Murrow, a great personal hero, but he's got nothing on what we, as a network, fuck Murrow! I mean, fuck him, he's not the only one who ever achieved greatness in television news. He's not the only one! Right? There is a legacy here that I am in awe of. And I mean, I feel deeply the responsibility. So this is all said in that context. This meeting is taking place in that context. I know you've been approached by CNN.

JENNIFER. No. Oh. No, that's –

WES. You don't have to deny it, this isn't, you're not –

JENNIFER. No, I – I mean it, I haven't spoken to anyone, Wes, honestly I haven't.

WES. Jennifer. You're not in trouble. That's what I'm saying. This is the context of our discussion, it's most important to me that you realize that. Other people under these circumstances, I'm not so sure I'd say that. But you're special. That's the context.

(He puts his hand on hers. She looks at it. After a moment, she puts her hand on top of his.)

JENNIFER. Thank you, Wes. I appreciate your saying that.

*(They look at each other. **WES** nods.)*

WES. I appreciate your saying that too. And I want you to think and listen to what I'm telling you now. What they are doing, over there at CNN, what they've enabled themselves to do, is to marry the highest level of journalistic professionalism with a profitability unheard of in today's market. It's very, very seductive, that combination. You probably don't spend a lot of time thinking about things like profitability; you're an artist, a reporter, same thing. I'm the head of the network. I think about it all the fucking time. And even though CNN has a lot to offer? For an artist like you? We can protect you in ways –

JENNIFER. Wes, please, I'm just not –

WES. Jennifer, I'm giving you every chance to play your cards right here. You know, and I know, I want you. The network wants you. You need to know that.

JENNIFER. I…do know that.

WES. What do you want, Jennifer?

JENNIFER. I'm pretty happy where I am, Wes.

WES. That's not what I'm asking.

JENNIFER. Isn't it?

WES. Jennifer, don't talk to me like I'm an idiot –

JENNIFER. I'm not! Oh god, Wes – my loyalty is here. My loyalty is to you.
(*beat*) I'm not unaware of the heat. I know, of course, I know that things are going to change. I know that. But, I don't need you to make me any kind of counteroffer.

WES. That's not what your agent tells me.

JENNIFER. Wes, I don't know what he said. But if he told you, if he, if he –

WES. No, no, Jennifer. You're not in trouble. He is ambitious for you. As he should be. He knows what he has.

JENNIFER. I just don't want you to think, in any way, that I would be disloyal to the network. I consider this my home. And you are, I admire you so much.

WES. I want to protect you, Jennifer.

JENNIFER. That's what I want, Wes. I want to be here. This network is what I want.

(*He kisses her. She falls into his arms. They start to make out.*)

(**ALICE** *watches* **MERV** *watch television. The television murmurs.*)

MERV. Oh that is so bogus. Cut it out! Asshole. What a fucking asshole.

ALICE. What are you watching?

MERV. It's this reality show. These people, they live in this house – boy, she is just a piece of work, this girl Sienna, she like thinks everyone is in love with her, she's just like this total fat cow and she's constantly coming onto everybody in the house. Like totally oblivious to reality, plus she thinks she's so fucking fascinating she can't shut up about the most mundane fucking shit, you just want to kill yourself listening to this MORON, God I'm sick of her. Why don't they get rid of her? I'm sick of this, I am so sick of this!

ALICE. What is it again?

MERV. It's this show, I told you, a reality – these people live in this –

(off T.V.)

What? What?

ALICE. What?

MERV. *(distracted)* These people live in this house, and they do things you know, and then people vote about who should get kicked out. It's hard to explain.

ALICE. Uh huh.

MERV. *(laughing, off T.V.)* Oh, god. That is so lame. You are fucking lame Sienna! You are so gone gone gone! You are out, mamacita, your ass is out of here!

ALICE. You know, there's this section of Vermont, that I lived in last summer, where you can't get television. This is a true story. I don't know why, but they can't get television.

MERV. They don't have T.V. in Vermont? Cut it out.

ALICE. I don't think it's everywhere, in Vermont, but I think it's a couple places.

MERV. I don't believe you.

ALICE. It's true. I was there.

MERV. What were you doing there?

ALICE. I was working on an organic farm.

MERV. Okay, well that's why there was no television, because you were on some hippie commune that didn't believe in it. It's not that you couldn't get it.

ALICE. No, you couldn't get it.

MERV. That's nuts.

ALICE. You can't really get radio either, so you'd be surprised, how much you get done. I mean, the only thing to do? Is stuff that needs to be done. It was like a disease, a disease of productivity.

MERV. Yeah, okay –

ALICE. And you read books and shit?

MERV. Ha ha.

ALICE. Because it was like freedom, like being a free person living in America. Because there was no television.

MERV. You suck.

ALICE. I don't suck. De Tocqueville said this thing – 'cause I was reading books, you know, while I was up there I actually read *Democracy in America* –

MERV. *(overlap)* Oh God Alice I mean you are not my mother, you're not actually my girlfriend either, much as you might like to be –

ALICE. *(overlap)* This is like bullshit, Merv –

MERV. *(overlap)* Because I know you have a total crush, but you're going to have to get that under control –

ALICE. You sitting her here and watching this crap – it's like the opposite of independence –

MERV. Because I hate to be the one to inform you, you're not really my type –

(He ups the volume on the T.V.)

ALICE. There is no liberty here, not to mention intelligence, this is the opposite of the American dream!

MERV. Hey, here's a clue! The total fucking shrew thing isn't actually what's going to get you into my pants!

(GRIGSBY drags herself out of one of the bedrooms, she is wearing crumpled surgery scrubs.)

GRIGSBY. Listen, could you guys keep it down

ALICE. You can't even have a fucking conversation whenever that thing is blaring –

GRIGSBY. *(exhausted)* I just did a thirty-six hour shift and I have another one in –

ALICE. I want this shit out of my house! And if I can't get it out of my house –

GRIGSBY. *(overlap)* Oh man, I am so slammed.

*(She goes. The front door opens and **VINCE** enters, dressed in a kind of crummy business suit. He tries to play mediator.)*

VINCE. *(overlap)* Whoa whoa whoa hey what is this – Alice, dude –

ALICE. *(overlap)* THEN YOU AT LEAST HAVE TO FUCKING TURN IT OFF ONCE IN A WHILE, YOU FUCKING LOSER!

(She mutes the T.V. herself.)

MERV. Like I said, Alice, you're not really for me but I do understand there are some tubercular homeless schizophrenics in the neighborhood who might be willing to give you a whirl.

ALICE. You are so fucking lowest common denominator, I can't believe that the planet actually wastes AIR on you.

MERV. Yeah, there's one with psoriasis who particularly might be desperate enough to want to date you.

(He laughs to himself at the cleverness of this. She looks at him, cold.)

ALICE. *(beat)* If you don't fucking clean up the kitchen by the time I get home, I swear to you I will cut your fucking heart out with a pair of nail clippers.

*(She goes. **MERV** looks at **VINCE**.)*

VINCE. Dude.

MERV. I did not start it.

VINCE. Sure, okay. You could clean the kitchen though, right?

MERV. Is it my turn? Because I lose track. I'm constantly cleaning it from my point of view but if it's like my turn I'm on it.

VINCE. I don't know whose turn it is.

MERV. That's my point. But I'll do it. I can do it right now.

VINCE. Great.

JENNIFER. In Beirut today –

(As **VINCE** *goes,* **MERV** *stays where he is, turns the television up loud.* **JENNIFER RAMIREZ** *on the set.)*

– terrorists exploded two car bombs in front of the American Embassy, killing four and wounding sixteen Lebanese citizens, while in Baghdad sixty-one Muslims died when suicide bombers infiltrated a shite mosque during evening prayer.

*(***STU** *enters, asking a question to someone off.)*

STU. How much do I have? Two minutes?

(then, to **JENNIFER***)*

Fantastic, Jennifer, you look great. It's going great.

JENNIFER. There's something wrong with the copy today, this doesn't sound right.

STU. You okayed it this morning. Listen –

JENNIFER. It's just not lively, there's no punch to it. Who wrote this?

STU. It's the same team of writers we've been using, but that's not –

JENNIFER. No, it doesn't sound right. What is this "shite" mosque, a shite mosque – oh fuck, fuck me, did I say that? Tell me I didn't say that.

STU. You sounded great.

JENNIFER. Can we loop it?

STU. Well, the show is live.

JENNIFER. I just said "shite mosque" on national television.

STU. It's six in the morning, no one is watching.

JENNIFER. I said "Shite mosque!"

STU. It happens to everyone, you have to have a sense of humor about stuff like that. You're doing great.

JENNIFER. I'm sorry.

STU. It's fine.

(to tech personnel, off)

Yes, I'm aware, we're aware –

JENNIFER. It's just –

STU. It's fine. Listen, Wes asked me –

JENNIFER. Wes, you spoke to Wes?

STU. Yeah, I did, actually, I did.

JENNIFER. So what did he say?

STU. He wants to talk to you after the show.

JENNIFER. After the show?

STU. Yeah, he asked me to come tell you he needs to see you in his office. Right after the show.

JENNIFER. He's here? He's on this coast?

STU. He got in on the red eye.

JENNIFER. Is he in the building? Or in his limo? Did he see that? Is he watching the feed?

STU. I doubt it.

JENNIFER. Why not? Why wouldn't he be?

STU. I mean, I'm sure he's watching the feed. The likelihood is that he saw every minute.

JENNIFER. Then he saw that.

STU. Unless he missed it.

JENNIFER. Oh great now I'm upset. I'm upset. I'm upset.

STU. At the very least what we do know, is he's watching the feed now.

JENNIFER. I'm fine!

STU. That's good.

(He goes. She turns to the camera.)

JENNIFER. We'll have more on developments in the Middle East later in this morning's broadcast. But first, a word from our correspondent in Berlin here to report on the legacy of punk: fall fashion trends in Europe!

(She freezes while the camera switches over to the correspondent in Berlin. In his office, WES preaches to STU.)

WES. I'm just thinking about synchronicity. Branding. What do viewers come to this network for, people need to have an answer to that question and the answer needs to cross pollinate, it needs to breed, across time and space. Just kidding about the time and space, but not really. What do people come to us specifically, for? And I'm not talking about the past, we were the fucking Oldsmobile of networks for how long, your father's car, screw that, who the fuck wants to drive their father's fucking car? I want to drive a fucking Ferrari! That's what I'm talking about, driving a FERRARI, not – oh boy.

(He tosses the papers to the floor, his mood shifting.)

What the fuck is this stuff, this isn't, there's nothing NEW here, this shit is so lame, I don't want the same old fucking sitcom, and the same old fucking doctor shows, these fucking WRITERS, isn't there one person out there who has an original idea in his fucking head?

(He picks up the phone.)

Yeah can I talk to, who's the head of what is this shit I just got handed. Drama, comedy, who the fuck is – 'Scripted Programming.' That's right, who's that person. Don't tell me her name. I give a shit about her fucking name. Call her and tell her she's fired. No I don't want to talk to her about what else is in the fucking pipeline! Pipeline? Did you just say pipeline? Who the fuck is this? You're fired too. Both of you, you're both FIRED. Fuck!

(He hangs up.)

Sorry, I'm sorry but this ship is in fucking trouble. I don't need idiots talking to me about pipelines.

STU. I need to talk to you about Jennifer, Wes.

WES. Jennifer? She's phenomenal. What a gorgeous girl. I've been watching the rushes on her, she eats the camera. She eats it. I love her.

STU. *(plain)* Yeah, I love her too. She's great, the early show everybody's, if you're happy –

WES. Do I look happy? I'm fucking out of my mind, I am no I'm miserable, I just think she's an amazing girl. Why you got a problem?

STU. Not if you're happy.

WES. I told you I'm –

STU. – with her, if you're happy with Jennifer, that's all we care about. Because we think she's phenomenal. She's waiting in the outer office.

WES. She's here?

STU. Uh, yes, you called me at four AM and asked to see her, after the broadcast, you asked me to tell her –

WES. Christ I'm a moron, I called, of course I called, you must think I'm insane.

STU. Not at all.

WES. Bring her in, god, bring her in!

(STU *goes.* WES *is alone for a moment.* JENNIFER *enters with* STU.)

JENNIFER. Wes hi it is so great to see you! I didn't know you were on this coast –

WES. Just got here, just in time to catch the broadcast.

JENNIFER. Oh. Well. I wish I had known you were going to be here, we've been having some trouble with the copy, there's a couple of writers who I'm trying to be decent about it but it's just not clicking, so this morning, there was this piece about a, a mosque I don't know if you saw it but I just was not happy with the copy. At all.

WES. Yeah I saw that it seemed fine to me but now that you mention it there was something off. I know what you were talking about, it was –

JENNIFER. The copy was just not right. And I try to cover that stuff, I know it's up to me to proof what I'm reading, but –

STU. It's the same guys we've always used, Wes.

JENNIFER. Yes you said that Stu but –

WES. Well fire 'em.

JENNIFER. Oh. I –

WES. They're no good, you should be happy, fire 'em.

STU. All of them?

WES. That piece sucked. Who wants to hear Jennifer Ramirez talking about mosques and Iraq and it's just crap, fire them.

JENNIFER. No, I don't think –

WES. You don't think what? *(beat)* Stu, could we have a moment?

STU. Sure Wes.

(He goes. **JENNIFER** *and* **WES** *are left alone.)*

JENNIFER. I wish I had known you were coming.

WES. You said that before.

(He starts to undress her.)

JENNIFER. Oh god…I have an appointment with a producer about a segment on homeless children…we're supposed to be at a shelter on the lower east side; Okay, in half an hour…some of them are living in the subway tunnels…

WES. God you're amazing…keep talking…

(He continues to undress her, lay her down on the table and climb on top of her as she continues to talk.)

JENNIFER. Two kids got electrocuted last week when they jumped on the third rail to get away from an oncoming train and the city covered the whole thing up… they're saying the MTA is looking at a sixty million dollar lawsuit if it gets out…

WES. Don't stop.

JENNIFER. More than twenty percent of the nation's children...will be living under below the poverty line in the next decade...half of them will be homeless...

(WES comes, collapses on her.)

GRIGSBY. Get this. So this asshole, I've already covered for him twice –

(In their kitchen, MERV and GRIGSBY are raiding the refrigerator. GRIGSBY is again in scrubs. VINCE is there, having a beer.)

– he shows up drunk – I'm not kidding – for his call DRUNK and he's puking in the men's room.

VINCE. Okay but one has to ask what were you doing in the men's room, Grigsby?

GRIGSBY. Saving this fucking idiot's life. This dude is supposed to be a DOCTOR, I kid you not, he's expecting people to put their lives in his hands, when he's sober at least, which is practically never these days –

MERV. God there's nothing to eat around here. Yogurt, are you kidding me? Is this yogurt or is it what is it?

(He keeps looking around.)

GRIGSBY. So he's puking in the men's room and he's supposed to be scrubbing up, right?

VINCE. I know, there aren't even any crackers.

MERV. I know.

VINCE. How come there are never any crackers?

GRIGSBY. I'm not kidding he's supposed to assist on this surgery –

VINCE. Like a fucking Triscuit –

MERV. I know there's nothing to eat around here.

VINCE. I'm going to go get some Triscuits. You want anything?

MERV. Triscuits.

(VINCE goes.)

GRIGSBY. *(overlap)* Okay, it's a stomach stapling, nothing earth shattering, but dude, your hands have to be clean and you're not allowed to puke in this person's stomach, you know what I mean?

MERV. Oh gross, you know, that is –

GRIGSBY. I know, but it could happen! Don't eat that, Alice will throw a fit if you eat that, she has to go to a special store to get that. So, I'm going dude, you have to get out of here, no one can see you, if the resident or one of the nurses, anybody sees you, your whole career is over. Like, over. I'm not kidding Merv, don't eat that, you won't like it anyway and you'll just piss her off.

MERV. I'm hungry.

GRIGSBY. Well go out and buy some food for once. Or just even leave it alone, Vince just went out for Triscuits!

MERV. We do the food together, I'm allowed to eat the food!

GRIGSBY. "We do the food together," when was the last time you –

MERV. So what happened with this dude? The drunk who was puking into someone's, like open –

GRIGSBY. No, he didn't, that's what I'm saying, I got him out of there and totally covered for him, I did. His shift on top of my own. Like the second time this week. I'm completely shot, I mean I am utterly slammed within an inch of my life and I'm like, why? Why do I do it? Why don't I just let this idiot hang himself, figuratively, he's a horrible doctor, I can't imagine that he's ever going to get any better. Why am I ruining my health to protect this moron?

MERV. You want to sleep with the guy?

GRIGSBY. No, god he's a disgusting alcoholic pig.

MERV. Bleck, what is this shit?

GRIGSBY. I told you, that's the yogurt Alice – why did you eat that? You know she's going to throw a fit and now you're just throwing it away!

MERV. Well it tastes like shit.

GRIGSBY. Jesus Merv you know you're not a total moron. You're just deliberately provoking her all the time –

MERV. I wanted something to eat and then I didn't like it –

GRIGSBY. Oh for god's sake you can take that position but I sat here and told you –

MERV. I was listening to your story.

GRIGSBY. You were not listening, if you were listening you would have stopped eating the yogurt when I told you to.

MERV. *(overlap)* I was – hellloo, excuse me, I was in fact listening to your story, that was completely the focus of my interest here –

GRIGSBY. *(disgusted)* What is wrong with the men on this planet?

MERV. That's a lovely thing to say. You must be taking charm lessons from our good friend Alice.

GRIGSBY. Just do me a favor and replace it would you?

MERV. Replace what?

GRIGSBY. The yogurt! I don't want to have to listen to another complete and utter fucking conflagration between you and your nemesis, over absolutely nothing. So just replace it would you?

MERV. Replace it with what?

GRIGSBY. Replace it before she gets home and notices it's gone!

MERV. If she wants to make a big fucking deal over a fucking carton of yogurt –

GRIGSBY. Oh for god's sake. Replace it. Replace it. Replace –

MERV. I will, I'll replace it! God everyone is so high strung in this house. It's totally fucking ridiculous.

GRIGSBY. Just do it! Do it! Do it! Do it!

MERV. *(overlap)* I'm doing it I'm doing it I'm doing it!

(She goes. **MERV** *makes a face behind her back and picks up the clicker. He turns on the television set.)*

(JENNIFER *appears, talking to the camera.*)

JENNIFER. Do you have enough Vitamin A in your diet? How much is enough and how much is too much? Today we look at the controversy surrounding dietary supplements and their impact on your health. But first, a look at the weather.

(*She turns, tilts her head.* WES *watches, with* STU.)

WES. She's phenomenal.

STU. Listen, Wes, we need to talk about this reality thing.

WES. It's a sensational idea, right? Somebody in marketing came up with it, I can't even remember the guy's name, but she's going to be sensational.

STU. People in news are a little uncomfortable.

WES. What people?

STU. Just general, in discussion, there's been some discussion about the legitimacy factor. As the morning anchor, Jennifer is the face, one of the faces, of network news. If she also serves as the host of a reality television show, there's some feeling that that will undermine her credibility, you see, as a journalist.

WES. No, I don't see.

STU. Well, it's seen as a conflict between news and entertainment.

WES. A conflict how?

JENNIFER. Take your daughter to work day! Learn how one woman and her daughter turned a familiar ritual into something a little more lucrative. But first, a report on spring cleaning. When was the last time you reorganized your closets?

WES. Look at her. She's gold.

STU. I was just asked to pass on people's concerns.

WES. You keep saying "people," but you don't give up any names, Stu, what are these people afraid of?

STU. I wouldn't say afraid, Wes –

WES. You wouldn't? I would.

STU. I would say, concerned –

WES. Fuck you, stop waffling, what the fuck are people complaining about? She's a fucking star, we'd be crazy not to use her, people, whoever these people are can go fuck themselves. This is about branding. People want to know who we are as a network, well let me tell you, who we are is her.

JENNIFER. In today's broadcast we continue our look at household pets. Are tropical fish right for you? But first, a look at sports.

WES. Phenomenal.

STU. *(unflappable)* Our understanding, the way that marketing presented this, ah, move, to us, it seems that the idea is that she will host this reality show, "Our House," interview the contestants –

WES. They're not "contestants."

STU. It's not my field, Wes, I'm not sure of the terminology. The participants, say, she interviews them and presents the edited tape of events in the house each week, that's what her involvement would be?

WES. She's a star; I want to use her. I don't see the problem.

STU. There's a rumor that she'll be reporting on those events. On the morning news.

WES. As I said, I don't see the problem.

STU. The news division doesn't think that what happens on reality television is news.

WES. It's reality. Why shouldn't it be news.

STU. Hmmm. Okay. Yeah, I don't think they saw it that way.

WES. Who is they?

STU. Like I said, these are just some general responses, Wes. I don't think anyone wants to go on record as saying that it's a bad idea.

WES. You tell me who they are, Stu, or it's your head on a fucking platter. Who's pissing on this?

STU. Come on, Wes. Everybody loves Jennifer. These really are just questions about how it's all going to work. We want to make the transition as smooth for her as possible. We all want the same thing here. We want Jennifer to be as awesomely successful as she deserves.

JENNIFER. But first, let's hear who's in and who's out in *Our House.* Hi I'm Jennifer Ramirez. I'm joining you mid-season as the new host of this challenging, ground breaking and exhilarating competition. During their first weeks living together, we watched the various housemates get to know each other, developing likes and dislikes, alliances and animosities.

MERV. Jennifer Ramirez. I can't believe this. Jennifer Ramirez! This is so lame.

(He turns up the volume on the television and sits, happily entranced. ALICE *enters, sees the television set on, tenses up.)*

ALICE. Good evening Merv.

MERV. Alice hi, how are you today? Wow check her out. How much work has she had done? Nobody looks like that. Barbie looks like that. Malibu nosejob Barbie.

I mean I hate it when gorgeous women cut their hair like that, it's like I'm so beautiful I can cut it all off and look I'm still great looking, it's so aggressive. It's like look at me! Look at my bone structure! She probably hasn't had plastic surgery, I take it back. But she is so skinny, I don't believe it for one second. She probably spends half her life in the bathroom throwing up.

ALICE. Okay these ramblings about Jennifer Ramirez are truly fascinating.

MERV. They're not ramblings. It's my personal exegesis about the fetishization of the female form. I mean it's not like I'm, but it is, what is she doing on *Our House?* She's Miss Morning News! Except it's not the real news anymore it's Hi, let's talk about really stupid shit and pretend that you're like on a date with Jennifer Ramirez kind of news. Fucking retard. Wow is she pretty. I love this show. I just love it. It's so spectacularly trashy.

(ALICE mutes the television.)

ALICE. Great. Look, we have to have a house meeting this weekend to talk about bills and next year's lease.

MERV. Well, that's super, Alice. I'll really be looking forward to that.

(He reaches for the clicker, she takes it with her, casual, a couple steps away.)

ALICE. We're going to have to balance the books for the fiscal year, so everyone is going to have to rectify their house account. Is that going to be a problem for you?

MERV. It depends on what exactly you mean by "rectify your house account," Alice. To my unpracticed ear it sounds a little like you're trolling for sexual favors. But I have a feeling that's not what you think you're doing.

ALICE. No, the point I'm trying to make is a tad more financial. Here's what you owe.

(She hands him a sheet of paper.)

MERV. What I "owe"?

ALICE. What you owe, three months rent on the year, and there's what you owe on the groceries and the house expenses.

MERV. And what's this?

ALICE. Let's see what does it say? "Interest." That's the interest that you owe to the rest of us for carrying your debt for part of the year.

MERV. You expect me to pay interest. To you.

ALICE. I expect you to pay forty two hundred and seven dollars and sixty three cents, to the house account, on Saturday. If you can't pay that, we're going to have a discussion about whether or not you should be here, next year.

MERV. You're kicking me out! What the fuck, you think you're kicking me out of my own house?

ALICE. I'm not kicking you out, Merv –

MERV. You fucking bitch!

ALICE. Oh that's great –

MERV. You fucking think you're going to kick me out of my own house –

ALICE. I am just telling you the facts! If you are not able to keep up with your share of the house expenses you need to find a place you can afford!

MERV. This is my house, this isn't your house!

ALICE. It's not fair for you to expect me and Vincent and Grigsby to –

MERV. I moved in here with Laurel and Daniel and Phil long before any of you, you came to me, in case you've forgotten –

ALICE. This isn't who got here first, that's not the rule that you were here first so you get to do whatever you fucking want.

MERV. And you don't get to make up the rules as you go along! Merv got the good bedroom!

ALICE. You owe all of us a lot of money!

MERV. Merv watches television! I'm just too uptight to even have a conversation with Merv so I think I'll just make up a new set of rules to just kick Merv out –

ALICE. Could you please stop yelling? I cannot have a conversation with a person who is just yelling at me.

MERV. Stop acting like such a bitch and I'll stop yelling!

(There is a terrible pause at this. **ALICE** *takes a breath, shakes her head.)*

ALICE. We're going to meet here, at four, on Saturday. If you're not there, you're out.

(She turns to go.)

MERV. There's four of us. You'd need three votes to get me out. Because if you vote yes and I vote no, that's one on each side, and then if either Grigsby OR Vincent votes with me it's a tie. Did you think of that? Huh? You can't get me out unless it's unanimous! And you'll never get it, it doesn't ever work like that. You know what really happens when you try a power play like this? You're the one who ends up going. And that's on you. You're the one who put this on the table. You're going down.

ALICE. See you Saturday. You might want to put on some fucking pants.

(He turns, dismissing her, and clicks on the television set. **JENNIFER** *steps forward, happy.)*

JENNIFER. In today's show we get to find out who will prevail in the ongoing, tension-filled confrontation between Raven and Jimmy Jack. This week's challenge pitted house members against each other in a culinary fight to the finish in the battle of the Belgian Waffles!

MERV. Awesome.

*(***STU** *and* **WES** *watch, from his office.)*

WES. You think her hair looks all right? You don't think it's too short do you?

STU. Looks fine to me.

WES. I think it's kind of, I mean I love it, but in the Midwest you know what they're all saying. Lesbian! Lesbian!

STU. So what's the question? Do I think Jennifer looks like a lesbian?

WES. God no, we know she doesn't look like a lesbian. What about her breasts? I mean they're beautiful but a little more cleavage is never a bad thing. Don't they have bras with little pumps on them? We should look into that.

STU. I think she looks great.

WES. No arguments from me on that. She looks great, she is great. Nose might be too perfect. That's what they say in the chat rooms. Her nose is too perfect! What can I do? She's perfect. Giving two thousand per cent. Nevertheless, the numbers still suck.

STU. The numbers are good, Wes.

WES. Don't tell me the numbers are good Stu. I can't sell shit on the morning news, excuse me that's not true, I can sell slightly more shit, on the morning news, than I can on the evening news, but the going price for shit is shit. Christ. Americans like optimism. The news division bleeds money, I'm throwing everything I can at it, Jennifer Ramirez, the hottest anchor on the air, and I still can't pull it out of the red. Maybe if I had her, you know, take her clothes off while she was reading the copy. Just kidding but you know they did that in Europe and it got people to watch.

STU. I'm sure it did.

WES. I wouldn't do that but it would work.

STU. But you wouldn't do that.

WES. But I might fucking think about it. Christ! The fucking news. It's just a fucking loser, no matter what you do; it needs to be canceled altogether. You can't make it work? Then you cancel it. We are fucking canceling all of it.

STU. You can't cancel the news, Wes.

WES. What did you say? Did you say, "can't"?

STU. Wes, come on, it's in our contract with the FCC.

WES. The fucking FCC. You think I give a shit about the FCC? They're fucking morons!

STU. The network's contract with the FCC states clearly –

WES. Do not fucking lecture me about my own fucking network! Do you want to keep working here or not?

STU. My point being, Wes, that the airwaves, the deal we have with the government is that we get the airwaves for free.

WES. Nothing's for free in this country.

STU. Well, precisely. That's the deal. They give us the airwaves, we are required by law to present a certain number of hours a week, of news coverage.

WES. Well, then they should pay for it. Has anyone looked into this? The news division loses money hand over fist. You know why? Because nobody gives a shit about the news.

STU. I don't agree with you.

WES. You don't what?

STU. People care, people…want to know…the world…we don't want to be alone. We want to know…our neighbors.

WES. You're fired.

STU. God, Wes, no. I am not disagreeing with you, I see the force of your argument –

WES. You're fired!

STU. *(suddenly forceful)* But whether or not you're right doesn't matter! The fact is, we get the airwaves for free. In exchange for that, we have to provide news. Period. End of story. It's the law. You cannot – you CANNOT cancel the news.

And you can't, god, for that matter you can't dumb it down anymore, you've dumbed it down so far what's left of it mostly resembles a catfood commercial.

WES. Hey, I do what I'm forced to do. People like cats.

STU. PEOPLE NEED THE NEWS. And it is our social responsibility –

WES. Our WHAT?

STU. YES, no, no, yes we have a responsibility, it is a holy trust, you can't possibly think – god, I'm here every day performing this soul sucking sysphian defense of the notion that people deserve the news whether they want it or not because I believe in KNOWLEDGE and INFORMATION because that makes us different and better, yes, better than the lower primates or our our our pets! People need news. If we choose – if we only pump commercials and and and SHIT into their homes through the powerful and and completely unknowable instrument, the TELEVISION SET, if all we do is send out-SHIT – then then we are the ones. We are culpable. Of the destruction of the human race. I believe that I really believe that.

WES. So what you're saying is that the human race would be more important to you than the numbers.

STU. What I'm saying is if you try and cancel the news they'll turn on your girlfriend.

WES. Watch yourself.

STU. *(ignoring the warning)* They're always looking, you know this, they're always looking for an excuse to turn. If you try to fly in the face of the rules on something this big? She's the one they'll go after. They'll go after both of you together. Wes put too much faith in Jennifer Ramirez.

WES. Fuck you.

STU. Wes' paramour couldn't handle it.

WES. I'm telling you.

STU. Wes put his faith in the wrong anchor. He was thinking with his dick and that's why the news division is –

WES. Don't fucking push it.

STU. I'm fired, Wes. I'm the most useful person you have right now.

(beat)

WES. Go on.

STU. There's nothing you can do about the news division. Leave it alone.

WES. CNN charges for news! Why can't I charge for news!

STU. Because you get the airwaves for free. CNN pays –

WES. Oh fuck CNN, I give a shit about CNN, the self righteous shitheads. I'd like to feed Anderson Cooper to the Israelis, they'd know what to do with him.

(silence)

You know, before he was all Anderson Cooper, he was the host of the Mole. The Mole! You know that. You know that.

STU. I didn't know that.

WES. It's true. The internet. How come that's not airwaves? What is it anyway? How come no one has to pay for that?

STU. They do, actually.

WES. They do?

(Both are silent for a moment. **STU** *cautiously continues.)*

STU. Yes. And CNN –

WES. I got it, Stu; I got it.

(There is another pause.)

STU. I'll go clear out my desk.

WES. What? Why?

STU. You fired me.

WES. Oh for fuck's sake, you're not fired. Somebody's got to run that loser news division. Lose any more money and you ARE fired. No. No. Say anything shitty about Jen? Ever again? Ever? And you're so fucking fired you will never work anywhere again. I will see to it that no one on earth will hire you to clean their toilets, that's how fucking fired you will be.

STU. Understood.

WES. Good.

*(***JENNIFER*** *stands in a spotlight. She glows. She is beautiful.)*

JENNIFER. We're down to the last challenge. After tonight's battle, you the viewers will decide who the winner of *Our House* is going to be. But first, let's check in on how things stand.

*(***ALICE, GRIGSBY, VINCENT*** *and* **MERV** *gather around the kitchen table.* **ALICE** *has xeroxed pages which she hands around.)*

ALICE. Okay. Let's get this over with.

MERV. Get it over with, are you kidding? I was planning on savoring every second.

GRIGSBY. So what is this?

ALICE. It's the house books. This section is income, that would be everyone's monthly contribution –

MERV. Contribution? You mean all that money we give you is like a contribution –

VINCE. I can't read these things.

ALICE. It's a spreadsheet, Vincent, you look at them all the time at work, I'm sure.

VINCE. I don't look at them all the time at work, because I can't make head or tail out of them.

MERV. Well, I don't understand it. Vince doesn't understand it. So, putting you in charge of the books was maybe not the smartest thing we ever did because half of us can't figure out any of this and you expect us to make "contributions" when as you may or may not know, most of us are living on you know really limited incomes.

ALICE. Contribution was not the right word.

MERV. Well what is the right word? How are we supposed to –

GRIGSBY. *(snapping)* Would you knock it off, Merv? This isn't helping.

MERV. Oh, I didn't realize that I was supposed to help –

VINCE. *(reading)* Oh wait, I see. So this is the income, what's income to the house and this is expenditures?

ALICE. Yes. YES, everyone's monthly checks, as they are received, are here. So this is the sum we have to work with, for all the house expenses in addition to covering the rent – which are here. Electricity, water, heat, groceries –

VINCE. Miscellany, what's that cover?

MERV. Yeah, what the fuck is that?

ALICE. One-time expenses, the new shower curtains, the grill for the back porch –

MERV. Which no one uses.

VINCE. I used it last summer.

GRIGSBY. I use it.

MERV. Like three times maybe someone used it.

VINCE. *(off sheets)* So, we have, what do we have in the bank? Is this –

ALICE. Thirty-three dollars and twenty-seven cents.

VINCE. Not much of a cushion.

ALICE. Particularly not if we want to get the carpets cleaned and the bathrooms repainted, as we discussed.

MERV. When did we discuss that? I don't remember discussing anything.

ALICE. We discussed it –

MERV. I didn't discuss it. You want to use the extra money in the bank to clean the carpets? After no one uses the grill that was your big idea –

GRIGSBY. The grill was my idea.

MERV. Well, my idea, of what to do with the house fund, is to get a high definition television.

GRIGSBY. There's only thirty three dollars in the house fund, Merv, how are we supposed to pay for –

MERV. You can get them on credit, at Best Buy. Zero dollars down. You go in and you order it and they let you take it home, no payments necessary for the first six months.

ALICE. Look, could we stay on point here?

MERV. How is this off point?

ALICE. The real point is, that in fact the reason there is only thirty three dollars –

MERV. The point is, that people are interested in this proposal, about getting a high def television set –

ALICE. IS BECAUSE YOU, MERV, HAVE NOT PAID YOUR RENT AND EXPENSES FOR THREE MONTHS THIS YEAR. THE POINT IS THAT YOU OWE THE HOUSE MORE THAN FOUR THOUSAND DOLLARS. FOUR THOUSAND DOLLARS IS WHAT YOU OWE.

(There is a pause at this.)

GRIGSBY. Okay, could we dial this back a little bit?

ALICE. He does, he owes at least four thousand dollars.

VINCE. That much? Whoa, dude, you're that far behind?

(He looks at the papers in front of him.)

MERV. I'm not behind. I'm a little behind. But four thousand dollars, she's charging me all this crazy interest, she's totally inflated those numbers.

ALICE. The numbers are the numbers.

MERV. This is like a congressional budget, you can make the numbers say whatever you want them to say. I don't accept these numbers.

GRIGSBY. What do you mean you don't accept them?

MERV. Just what I said, I don't accept any of this.

ALICE. You –

VINCE. So what are you saying, that you did pay the money?

ALICE. He did not –

MERV. Of course I paid! If she lost the check –

ALICE. Oh I'm sure –

MERV. It is possible –

ALICE. It is not –

MERV. Oh, you're like infallible –

ALICE. Three checks. Three months. January, April, AND May.

(She goes through the papers, starting to shake a little.)

I sent out, when the checks did not come in, I put a reminder in your mailbox, by the door. These are copies for –

MERV. I've never seen this.

GRIGSBY. You've never seen one of these? Cause I got one, she put one in my box when I was a week late.

MERV. I've never heard anything about any of this.

ALICE. That is a lie, Merv –

MERV. And now you're calling me a liar!

ALICE. Yes, because you're lying!

VINCE. Look we really got to keep this dialed down or we won't get through it. If you owe this much money, dude – let's just say maybe, it's possible that the checks got lost –

ALICE. I did not –

VINCE. *(overlap)* OR THAT YOU FORGOT, and the reminders forms, for whatever reason, you didn't notice them –

MERV. I never got them!

VINCE. Whatever, what I'm saying here is, you know, four thousand dollars is a lot, that's –

MERV. She added interest.

GRIGSBY. The interest is like sixteen bucks, Merv.

VINCE. The point being, like, how long is it going to take you, to pay the house back?

ALICE. How long. How long?

VINCE. *(reprimanding her)* Would you just, Alice, look, we're all in this together and I'm just finding out about and I'd really love a chance just to hear what Merv thinks he can do about replacing the money. I mean, I didn't know about this, and I'm surprised frankly you let it get this far, without sharing it with the other members of the house.

MERV. Yeah.

ALICE. I told you, I did tell you he was behind.

VINCE. You did, yes you did. But we didn't know, obviously that things were this serious. So now we just need to take this one step at a time. Merv. Where are you financially?

MERV. Well, I was in better shape before I heard this.

VINCE. But you're working, right? There's income, you think you can pay this back?

MERV. Absolutely I can pay it. I was in between jobs a couple months ago, I don't know if you are aware, this is a terrible economy, but yeah, I do have like three part time things that are coming up. One starts next week. I just don't have a ton of extra cash, just lying around my bank account.

VINCE. How much do you have?

MERV. Off the top of my head? A couple three thousand.

VINCE. So maybe you can pay half of this –

MERV. Absolutely, two thousand, right away –

ALICE. He –

VINCE. And then maybe make the rest up five hundred at a time? Is that going to be too big a stretch?

MERV. No, that's doable.

VINCE. An extra five hundred a month for, what is that, four months –

MERV. That sounds like a plan, sure.

VINCE. Okay. Okay. That okay with you guys?

ALICE. He isn't going to pay that back.

VINCE. Okay, so it's not okay with Alice. Grigsby –

GRIGSBY. Yeah, fine, if Merv pays the two thousand back by you know, when? Monday?

MERV. Monday?

VINCE. If it's there, dude, it's there, and if it's not, it's not. Is it there or not?

MERV. Of course it's there.

VINCE. Wednesday then. Okay, what else?

ALICE. I'm not okay with this.

MERV. *(under his breath)* Of course you're not.

ALICE. This has been an ongoing situation. He, I did, in fact, this doesn't have anything to do with the economy, he, you guys know that when someone forgets to pay their monthly check, I, I did put the reminders in, I did let him know, that he was, this is not, I don't have faith that he has the money or if he does, I believe he's going to, and besides which, BESIDES which there are other issues as well, this television thing –

MERV. Okay, maybe in the fantasy land of Vermont where everyone is too busy making cheese, nobody watches television. But I live in reality land where we have television!

ALICE. What does that even mean? Bullshit! Bullshit just comes out of your mouth and you act like it's true!

MERV. It's not bullshit, everything I say is true!

ALICE. It's BULLSHIT!

VINCE. OKAY –

GRIGSBY. You guys –

MERV. Okay, you are like the last person in America who thinks that T.V. is like the devil –

ALICE. I don't think that T.V. is the devil, but I reserve the right to say it should not be on all the time, blasting all the time –

VINCE. Yeah okay, there are some personal issues here we all know about, but we do need to keep things separate.

ALICE. But they aren't separate. They aren't separate. The money thing is ongoing. The television thing is a harassment, that is how I experience, it's just bombarding, all the time, and you can't connect. How can you have an actual conversation with anyone, when that thing is on, it interferes with everything, with life, you can't, people can't – connect – I am not crazy to want that! Plus, plus, my things are disappearing –

VINCE. Whoa, things are disappearing? Are you accusing, what are you saying?

ALICE. I'm saying, things are, food, my food, disappears and is not replaced –

VINCE. Oh, food...

ALICE. Yes, food that I eat, that is mine, my my my cereal, ice cream, nuts –

GRIGSBY. Those are household nuts, Alice, aren't they? I thought – I mean, I think I ate the nuts –

ALICE. My yogurt. Is gone. My, the Greek yogurt that I have to go halfway across town to get –

GRIGSBY. Oh, brother.

ALICE. Oh brother what! Did you eat that, too?

GRIGSBY. No, actually, I didn't. Merv ate the yogurt.

VINCE. *(a beat)* You ate the yogurt, dude?

MERV. *(a beat)* I was hungry.

ALICE. I knew it.

MERV. I didn't know. I thought it was, you know, household yogurt.

ALICE. Even if it was household yogurt you don't pay for that either!

MERV. Whoa, Alice...

GRIGSBY. Well, besides, I did tell you, Merv. You did know.

MERV. Did I? I...sorry. I guess I wasn't paying attention. I'm sorry, Alice. I guess I ate your yogurt.

VINCE. *(beat)* Is that it?

ALICE. No. That's not it. I want him out of here. This isn't working out, he can't – he's got to go. I cannot live with him. He has to go.

(beat)

VINCE. Well, I'm sorry you feel that way. I personally, uh, I'm not comfortable just tossing Merv out of the house, especially when he owes us four thousand dollars. Like, why would he feel like he should pay us back if we just kicked him out?

MERV. I wouldn't.

VINCE. Yeah. That's what I thought. So, I don't think it's a good idea.

ALICE. He...Grigsby...

GRIGSBY. Well, I don't think, okay. Look, I think I'm around a little more than Vince? So I agree with um Alice that there are some problems. I think we could maybe do with less T.V., and you know, be a little more respectful about the food things. I'd really like to know that Merv is going to try a little harder to respect you know Alice's boundaries, especially in those issues.

MERV. Is she going to respect my boundaries?

GRIGSBY. I think we should all respect each other's boundaries. That's what I think.

ALICE. I think he should go.

MERV. Well...I don't know what to say. Nobody else thinks that. So. Is that it?

VINCE. That seems to be it.

MERV. Great.

(He stands to go.)

GRIGSBY. Listen, that check?

MERV. Wednesday, right?

GRIGSBY. Yeah, but could you give it to Vince? Because if you say that Alice has been losing them, and Alice says you don't give it to her…it just keeps it a little cleaner, maybe, if you give it to Vince.

MERV. Do you think I've been lying?

GRIGSBY. I didn't say that. No.

MERV. It's not what you say. It sounds like what you think.

GRIGSBY. I just think it keeps things cleaner. Vince?

VINCE. That sounds good. I get the check. Is that a problem?

MERV. Not at all. Sounds great. See you guys.

(He goes into his room. **ALICE** *stands there, bereft, pissed.* **GRIGSBY** *and* **VINCE** *look at her.)*

GRIGSBY. You okay? Alice?

ALICE. Why do you…you know I'm not making this up. Why did you just let him do that?

(a beat)

VINCE. You know…these household situations, they're not for everybody. Some people maybe do better on their own. Or like, with one roommate.

ALICE. That's what I'm saying! He doesn't, he can't, he doesn't belong, he's not someone who can live in in community!

VINCE. I wasn't thinking him.

ALICE. You want ME to move?

GRIGSBY. I don't know, Alice. You don't seem to like this. Why would you stay?

ALICE. Because I didn't do anything wrong!

GRIGSBY. Yeah, but you don't like it here. I mean, do you? Do you like living here?

(There is another beat, then –)

ALICE. I liked living in Vermont.

VINCE. *(simple)* What did you like about it?

ALICE. *(laughing a little)* There weren't very many people. And there was no television. And…it was so pretty there. Hills. And streams everywhere. Trees. I learned how to knit. I liked that. I always felt…like I was living, like I was living my life.

VINCE. Why did you leave?

ALICE. I don't know. It didn't feel real somehow.

VINCE. And St. Louis is realler?

ALICE. *(She laughs a little.)* Oh well.

VINCE. Look, you're fine. When you're not completely fucking crackers you're great.

ALICE. This is nice. This is what I'm talking about. It's just a relief to connect.

(MERV comes out of his bedroom, wearing a hoodie, and approaches the others.)

Oh Merv, listen.

(MERV pulls his hand from inside his hoodie, and reveals a gun. He points it at her. The others react. He shoots ALICE.)

GRIGSBY. Merv, Merv…

(Then turns the gun and shoots GRIGSBY, then points the gun at VINCE.)

VINCE. *(overlap)* Jesus God, don't Merv for god's sake don't, Merv don't don't don't –

(MERV just stands there with the gun. VINCE sees that he is not shooting anymore. He waits for a moment.)

Okay. Okay, things are, you're not, just don't, um, okay, it's okay Merv. Why don't you just – just um, tell me what you want and we'll take care, take care of that. What do you want, what do you want, Merv?

(a beat)

MERV. I want to talk to Jennifer Ramirez.

(blackout)

End Act One

ACT TWO

(WES *talking to his board of directors.*)

WES. The fact is – I am told – the reality is – that we are required by the FCC to broadcast a certain number of hours of news, to the public, in exchange for the right to use the airwaves. Now. Clearly, I didn't make the rule up! No one checked in with me, when they invented America. And do I object to this rule, this so-called "law of the land"? I do. Why? Because staying informed, in America, is optional. No one forces anyone to read the newspaper! And they are consequently, blessedly, being permitted to fold, to go the way of the buggy whip and the penny whistle. It's not required to watch the evening news! Americans are free. Airwaves are free. How do those two fundamental truths add up to a requirement to broadcast the news? I ask, and ask, and ask. And no one answers.

(a beat)

There is a fundamental mistake here. Television, in its inception, seemed to present itself as a tool for humanity's further development, offering profound opportunities for communication, education, entertainment. But as time passed, and we became aware of its true nature, the tragic misunderstandings which surrounded these assumptions revealed themselves. Television is not our subject; it is not our creation! We are not looking at it! It is looking at us! And if we are real-I mean, if we are real – then television is what makes us real. Because it is hyper-real. And hyper-reality is not free. It's really expensive to run a network! And you know what is NOT optional, in America? Profitability. When the FCC and its misunderstandings and misconceptions about what television is, get in the way of our profits, I say: we stand up. And demand our rights. So. We're cutting seven hundred jobs out of the news division. There will still be news! But it will be news on our terms. Airwaves are free. Americans are free. The news is not free.

(applause)

(JENNIFER, getting ready to go on. She wears a red cowl neck sweater and she is flipping out while STU broods.)

JENNIFER. This is fucked. What is this? Is this a cowl neck? Who the fuck sent a cowl necked sweater to the set today?

STU. Wardrobe insists that they're really hot right now.

JENNIFER. I look like a fucking beefsteak tomato. That's not fucking hot. That's fucking, you're fucked, is what that fucking is.

(JENNIFER rips the red sweater off her.)

STU. You are aware that that is the twenty-fourth sweater you have rejected this morning.

JENNIFER. Don't talk back to me!

STU. I wouldn't dream of it. I'm just reporting the numbers.

(taking sweater)

Twenty-four. That's two dozen sweaters that you have rejected.

JENNIFER. Yeah, well we will go through six dozen fucking sweaters if we have to because this is fucking bullshit! Who the fuck is Katie Couric's wardrobe person, that's what I want to know. She looks like shit anyway. I am not going out there looking like shit. I don't care if you do think I'm acting like some sort of diva.

STU. No Jennifer no. I wouldn't say you're acting like a diva. I'd say you're acting like a cunt. Sorry, sorry...

JENNIFER. Fuck you. Where the fuck is Wes?

STU. *(disinterested)* He's giving a speech to the stockholders.

JENNIFER. Fuck the fucking stockholders! What the fuck is this shit all over my hands, what is this? It's red, it's red...

(She is rubbing her hands.)

STU. It's angora, it sheds.

JENNIFER. *(rubbing her hands)* I'm the face of news on this network. I AM the news. And I am not, I am not... GOING OUT THERE LOOKING LIKE A FUCKING TOMATO. I am the news. Katie Couric can go fuck herself. She's too fucking cute, the news isn't CUTE.

(She rubs her hands.)

WHAT THE FUCK IS THIS STUFF?

STU. It's angora.

JENNIFER. Fuck you, you're fired. Call wardrobe. I want them all fired. This is crap. THEY'RE ALL FIRED.

(The phone rings. STU answers it.)

STU. Yeah?

JENNIFER. You're fired Stu.

STU. Really?

(on phone)

Oh, she's fine.

JENNIFER. You're fired. Everybody – I'm the news. I'm the only –

STU. Right now?

JENNIFER. I used to be real. I did real news! I interviewed Koffi Annan. I interviewed Mel Gibson! Fuck Wes. I'm not doing anymore fucking reports on tropical fucking fish and apple martinis. Motherfucker. Goddamn fucking cocksucker. Don't tell him I said that.

STU. Well, she's a little busy.

JENNIFER. I can't, I can't – I can't – Let me talk to him. I don't want to talk to him. Did he hear that? Let me talk to him.

(STU hangs up.)

STU. Jennifer. Something's happened.

JENNIFER. I'm fired, right? I'm fucking fired well FUCK HIM. He can't fire me. I AM THE NEWS.

STU. You're not fired.

JENNIFER. I'm not?

STU. No. That was – something has happened.

(beat) There's a hostage situation. In St. Louis. Some idiot shot his roommates and now he wants to talk to you.

JENNIFER. He wants to talk to me, why does that make him an idiot?

STU. I don't think he's an idiot because he wants to talk to you. That's not what I meant. Although I understand why you might think I thought that. Or why other people might think I thought that.

JENNIFER. So who is this guy?

STU. It's hard to say. They think he might be a graduate student. Or a postal worker.

JENNIFER. And he wants to talk to me? *(beat)* Could we do it on the air?

(WES joins them, his office, where JENNIFER makes her case.)

WES. What is this? A graduate student? Who gives a shit about a graduate student?

JENNIFER. He might be a postal worker.

WES. You said graduate student.

JENNIFER. *(thrilled)* There are hostages, Wes, who may or may not be dying.

WES. You know about this?

STU. I just talked to the affiliate, we haven't even heard from the cops yet. If they do contact us I imagine it would at the most be some sort of teleconferencing situation although I can't imagine that they're even going to let her get involved that far –

JENNIFER. *(overlap)* No no no I want to go in! I got to be in there! I'm going to go in!

STU. They're most certainly not going to let her go in.

JENNIFER. I want to go in!

WES. You want to go talk to this graduate student?

JENNIFER. He asked for me, Wes. He didn't ask for Diane or Katie or Campbell Brown, or Soledad, or Christiane Amanpour, he didn't want any of them! He wanted me.

WES. Of course he wanted you. Everyone wants you. I want you.

STU. They have not asked for her to go in there.

JENNIFER. I want to go! I want to go!

WES. There are guns?

JENNIFER. Yes there are guns.

WES. Many guns?

STU. We haven't even talked to the cops yet!

WES. I don't know, Jen.

JENNIFER. Dan Rather went into Afghanistan!

WES. Yes he did and he looked really stupid with that thing on his head.

JENNIFER. I can do this, Wes.

STU. *(forceful suddenly)* You CAN'T do it. This is not – this isn't and besides which you're not, you're NOT –

JENNIFER. *(cold)* I'm not WHAT.

(There is a moment.)

STU. There are so many problems with this proposition I don't even know where to start. I can't, you don't, okay for one you do not negotiate with terrorists. You don't – most especially you don't send in – to negotiate with terrorists, you don't do it.

WES. Is he a terrorist or a graduate student or a postal worker, I'm not clear on this –

STU. He's a fan, Wes, instead of asking for her autograph he shot his roommates! It's some crazy sociopath who watches a lot of television. This isn't news this is, well I don't know what it is but she can't, this isn't – you can't –

WES. You know, Stu, every time you talk to me about the news I get nothing but negativity. What it isn't. What I can't do. I need you to stop telling me what the news isn't. It ISN'T tropical fish, although I got to say I liked that segment and a lot of people watched it. It ISN'T Jennifer Ramirez –

STU. I never said –

JENNIFER. He said that?

STU. I never said that.

JENNIFER. You said that?

STU. Jennifer! He would have fired me if I had said that!

JENNIFER. *(to* **WES***)* Did he say that?

WES. Nah, I just like it when you get all fiery and upset. Okay, so now we know what the news ISN'T. Maybe we should start considering what the news is or what it could be.

JENNIFER. That's what I'm saying.

(The blinds come up on the house.)

MERV. They got pictures of all of us!

*(***MERV***, watching television.* **ALICE** *and* **GRIGSBY** *bleeding on the floor.)*

Whoa, they got my picture from my driver's license, that sucks.

(He settles in to watch, happy.)

Picture of you too, it also sucks!

(laughing)

Dude, it looks like a high school prom picture, what is that you are wearing? Is that ruffles?

VINCE. *(on phone)* Yes sir. He is. Yes he is of course he does and he's waving it around!

*(***WES** *stands and paces, thinking about this.)*

WES. So this is happening in St. Louis? That's good.

MERV. That's quite a look.

VINCE. No he won't, he says –

WES. Middle of the country, the heartland.

MERV. I particularly like the boutonniere.

VINCE. He doesn't want to talk to you. He'll only talk to this newscaster, she's – I know but –

WES. People like that. More than the coasts at least.

VINCE. *(to* **MERV***)* They want to talk to you.

MERV. No! I already said only Jennifer, come on –

VINCE. *(repeating on phone)* He won't talk to you.

WES. I don't like it that he's a grad student. Sounds too much like "writer."

MERV. Oh, we're going live, excellent.

VINCE. No, no, sir.

MERV. So which cop is the one you're talking to? Can you come look at this and see?

WES. People don't give a shit about 'writers.'

VINCE. One is, Alice is unconscious.

JENNIFER. Maybe he's unemployed.

GRIGSBY. Merv, I got to talk to you.

WES. Unemployed is better.

GRIGSBY. Listen to me, Merv, are you listening to me?

MERV. You're loud and clear.

STU. They're not going to let her go in.

VINCE. No, sir I'm sorry I can't get him to do that!

*(***WES** *picks up the phone and dials.)*

GRIGSBY. Alice is in real trouble here.

MERV. She's fine.

WES. Yeah, it's me. Can you get me…

GRIGSBY. She's not fine, Merv. She's unconscious.

MERV. Oh, brother…

WES. Why don't you put me through to the governor of Missouri. Thanks.

*(***MERV** *bends over* **ALICE***, to check her breathing. It's not clear to him how she's doing.* **JENNIFER** *and* **STU** *with* **WES***.)*

VINCE. No, I'm not going to tell him that!

GRIGSBY. If we don't sit her up she'll drown in her own blood.

VINCE. Because I'm scared, that's why!

GRIGSBY. She'll bleed out faster, but at least she won't drown.

VINCE. Don't ask me that again. What he wants is this newscaster, Jennifer Ramirez, that's what he says he wants –

GRIGSBY. We have to get her help.

MERV. And pizza, ask for pizza.

VINCE. He'd also like some pizza.

GRIGSBY. Oh for fuck's sake

MERV. Pepperoni.

VINCE. Pepperoni if that's possible.

WES. Hi!

VINCE. Please could someone please just – they're both bleeding –

WES. I hear you have a situation in St. Louis.

GRIGSBY. At least let Vince help me move her.

MERV. Relax!

WES. Awful.

GRIGSBY. Vince!

WES. Just horrifying when these things happen. You have our sincere sympathy.

VINCE. Look, I got to go – I got to go!

MERV. No, No, No I'll do it.

（*He waves the gun at* **VINCE**, *who backs away.*）

WES. And I know that your men on the ground are doing everything they can. But I did hear that we might be able to help.

MERV. Helllooo. Alice?

VINCE. Look, could I please – they need me here, they need my help.

MERV. *(to* **ALICE***)* Are you in there?

VINCE. Can you please, I can't just sit on the phone and talk to you please –

*(***ALICE*** coughs.)*

MERV. She's coughing.

*(***ALICE*** coughs, again.)*

(to **GRIGSBY***)*

See.

GRIGSBY. We have to get her into a better position, Merv.

VINCE. Oh my god. She's dying. Please, please –

WES. Yes, that is what we heard. There might be some way for Jennifer to defuse –

JENNIFER. Yes!

STU. This is a mistake.

JENNIFER. Loser.

MERV. So, where are we at with the pizza?

WES. Uh huh. Uh huh.

GRIGSBY. Hang on sweetie, hang on.

VINCE. I have to go. I have to go.

WES. Well there's no question about that. It's the safety of those women that's paramount.

VINCE. Just get the pizza and get this stupid newscaster here! Now!

(He hangs up.)

MERV. Down, boy!

GRIGSBY. Vince –

VINCE. I know I know I know – Merv – you have to let me go to Alice –

WES. Great. I'll let her know.

(He hangs up.)

You're in.

JENNIFER. Wes!

(She throws her arms around him.)

(House phone rings.)

MERV. Vince are you going to get that?

VINCE. Oh God!

*(**MERV** gestures with gun for **VINCE** to answer.)*

WES. No no no. You can't be flip about this. This is real danger, Jen. This isn't television, this is real.

STU. I can't believe you just said that.

(She looks at him, surprised at his tenderness.)

VINCE. Hello, yes hello.

JENNIFER. Wes. This is about my integrity as a reporter. I have to do this.

WES. Baby.

JENNIFER. Wes. If this goes right? You and me? We will OWN the news. All of it. Everywhere.

(They kiss.)

WES. Let's go to wardrobe.

*(**MERV** pours his glass of water on **ALICE**'s head. She sputters, and moves.)*

VINCE. Alright!

GRIGSBY. Merv, please.

MERV. She's okay!

GRIGSBY. She's not okay, Merv, she needs to get to a hospital!

MERV. Look. I know this is serious. But I also know, from watching television a little bit about medical emergencies.

VINCE. Alright!

GRIGSBY. Yeah, not as much as me.

MERV. And Alice is not in great shape, okay, but she doesn't have a collapsed lung or anything.

GRIGSBY. Yeah, that's great but I am in fact a doctor, Merv – Merv – Merv – Christ –

MERV. *(overlapping)* So, I know you're in pain, and I respect that you want to get out of here? But, it's not like a serious medical emergency, Grigsby, I've seen too much *ER*, for that ploy to have any traction.

VINCE. That would be fine.

GRIGSBY. *(annoyed)* You don't watch *ER*. You watch reality television. Which looks NOTHING like REALITY so I don't know why they call it that.

MERV. I know, everybody thinks that.

VINCE. Yes. I will do that. Thank you.

(VINCE hangs up the phone.)

MERV. What'd they say?

VINCE. She's coming.

MERV. She's coming?

VINCE. Yes, Jennifer Ramirez is coming and and and when she gets here you have to let us go. Unless you want to let us go now.

MERV. Why would I do that?

VINCE. Because it might save Alice's life, Merv! Oh, forget it! I'm going to go help them. Don't shoot me.

MERV. I'm not going to shoot you. Would you stop acting like I'm a crazy person?

GRIGSBY. Vince, we need anything to stop the bleeding.

VINCE. *(off blood)* Oh shit. There's blood everywhere. Grigsby there's a lot of blood.

GRIGSBY. Just get every dish towel you can find.

(VINCE goes for a dishtowel, rips it up and starts to tie it higher above her arm.)

VINCE. If she dies, they will have you on murder charges, Merv! Murder one.

MERV. Listen to you with your murder one. You work in an office, fixing computer problems! What do you know about the legal system?

ALICE. *(coughing)* You guys…

GRIGSBY. God, Alice…

MERV. Nothing that you haven't seen on *Law and Order*, or *C.S.I.* –

ALICE. *(overlap, under)* I can't breathe.

GRIGSBY. *(overlap)* Vince, help me, we have to try and stem the bleeding even a little – ball the towels up as tight as you can and hold them against her chest. Don't let go.

MERV. *(continuing over)* – and I'm the one who's crazy, I love that.

VINCE. I'm going to Alice, Merv! Okay?

MERV. Yes, fine, whatever.

JENNIFER. Reporting live from the St. Louis hostage crisis, this is Jennifer Ramirez.

(She stands and goes to the center of the room, to report.)

Earlier today, an unemployed graduate student, Merv Masterson, allegedly shot two of his housemates, Alice Stiles, a legal secretary, and Dr. Sandra Grigsby, a second year medical intern at St. Louis Presbyterian Hospital.

MERV. *(overlap)* Hey, Vince, come take a look at this!

VINCE. I'm a little busy, Merv!

MERV. *(overlap)* She's out there! Jennifer Ramirez is out there!

JENNIFER. Our understanding is that the two women are wounded but alive inside the house and that local police officials have been negotiating with a third housemate to secure their release.

MERV. *(overlap)* She's reporting live in front of the house! Holy shit! In front of the fire truck! Why is there a fucking fire truck? We're not on fire.

JENNIFER. We take you inside the St Louis Hostage Crisis – live.

MERV. She's coming in. She's coming in. She's coming in.

VINCE. She's breathing different.

GRIGSBY. Hold her head to the side.

MERV. Boy this is awesome. This is more action than St. Louis has seen, like, ever. Whatever happened to that pizza.

(*Doorbell. Mutes T.V. A beat.* **MERV** *meets* **JENNIFER**.)

JENNIFER. Hi, I'm Jennifer Ramirez.

MERV. Oh, I know who you are. Come in, come in. It's just, wow, it's really a thrill to meet you, Jennifer. I've been a big fan for a long time. I mean, I am like addicted, as they can tell you, to *Our House.* I think it's just a fucking genius piece of television. And you are awesome, as the host? I don't care all the crap people write about you on the internet – I mean, I admit that I have participated in some of those chatrooms myself, so I don't want to pretend that I haven't had my quibbles with you and the show, you know, over time. I mean, I'd love to hear your perspective on those discussions. Because really even though we complain a lot, those of us who, you know, talk about the show, blog about it, whatnot, it's a sign of our passion, that's how I feel about it. Please, sit, sit! Can I get you something to drink?

JENNIFER. Sure, Diet Coke.

MERV. Do we have that?

GRIGSBY. It's Alice's.

MERV. So it's in the refrigerator.

JENNIFER. I think I'm fine, Merv. Can I set up the camera? Is that okay with you? That we broadcast this?

MERV. Yes. Please!

JENNIFER. I'm just going to set up right here then.

(*She sets up the camera.*)

VINCE. Hey. Hey! HEY.

(*Both turn and look at him.*)

What are you doing? We have to get– we have to get Grigsby and Alice out of here. They have to go to the hospital, now, Merv.

JENNIFER. Oh. You want to move them?

VINCE. That was the deal!

MERV. Actually, I think that was the deal, Jennifer.

JENNIFER. I'm sorry, that was not my understanding.

VINCE. That's why they let her in. That's why they let you in!

JENNIFER. My understanding is they let me in, to cover the story.

VINCE. This is the story. They're bleeding, she's bleeding, he shot them –

JENNIFER. And I'm here to bring that story to America. People want to know what is happening here. And that means, from all of you. But as a member of the press I am not permitted to interfere with events. It's like a, it's like ethics.

VINCE. Ethics?

JENNIFER. Like, if we were in a war, and I was embedded with an enemy platoon, maybe in Iraq, say, I would not be permitted to run away and alert our soldiers about what the enemy was doing. Because then I'd be a spy. And I'm not a spy. I'm a reporter.

VINCE. You know what? You should shoot me, Merv. Right now. YOU SHOULD FUCKING SHOOT ME RIGHT NOW, I AM BEGGING YOU.

MERV. I'm not going to shoot you.

VINCE. Would you please shoot me?

JENNIFER. I'm not saying you should not help them. That is not what I'm saying. I'm just saying that my actions cannot inform your actions. This is an interview. That is as far as I can go.

VINCE. What does that even mean?

MERV. Okay. This is what we'll do.

GRIGSBY. No no, no more negotiating Merv, Alice needs to get out of here now – her pulse is tready – I don't know how much longer I can keep her going.

VINCE. You have to let them go!

MERV. I will let them go! I said I would and I will, but it has to be after the interview.

(to JENNIFER*)*

Right?

JENNIFER. I can't tell you what to do.

GRIGSBY. No Merv, now now – now!

MERV. Come on as soon as I let them go the cops will come in and arrest me and then what about the interview? That doesn't really seem fair.

VINCE. Merv!

MERV. I'm just saying where we are, is where we are. I don't think it is really useful to keep going back to how we got here.

*(*ALICE *gasps for air.)*

VINCE. Hold on, honey hold on hold on –

JENNIFER. Look can I get this on tape?

GRIGSBY. *(overlap)* Fuck you!

MERV. Absolutely.

ALICE. I can't…

(She fades out.)

VINCE. Oh shit. Oh shit. You guys. Come on, you guys. She's maybe dying.

GRIGSBY. Merv, come on.

MERV. Look it's up to you. Do you want to keep arguing or do you want to quietly let us get through this so then you can get Alice some help.

GRIGSBY. Fuck you.

MERV. Is that a yes?

(to JENNIFER*)*

I think that's a yes.

JENNIFER. *(to camera)* Inside the St. Louis Hostage Crisis, I am Jennifer Ramirez. What we are watching is the aftermath of a horrific shooting in which two women were possibly mortally wounded –

(to **MERV***)*

JENNIFER. *(cont.)* Why don't you tell us what happened here, Merv. In your own words.

MERV. House dynamics are so hard to explain, Jennifer. I mean, people want things to be real simple. Like, he shot those women, he must hate his mother. But, honestly, we are, all of us, so much more mysterious than that.

JENNIFER. Let's go back to those house dynamics. There was conflict.

MERV. Yes but more than that too. I just think it's more like – life is like this huge field of of of chaos, and there are waves bombarding the heart and the mind constantly, waves of emotions, facts, events, people, desires-it's overwhelming and we're these television sets receiving the waves. Which are in the air everywhere – carrying everything, the world, into us, into our fragile, broken hearts, and then all of a sudden, you know, all of a sudden the television just – just just just just – just – just – a tube blows and that's it! And it's almost impossible to say why. Why, at that instant, there were too many you know ions or something.

JENNIFER. Then you think people are television sets.

MERV. Well – I – no, I was using a metaphor. You say 'A is B' when you really mean 'A is like B.'

JENNIFER. Did you learn about that in graduate school?

MERV. No, I think I learned about that in fourth grade from Mrs. Kline.

JENNIFER. Let's stay focused on your current situation. How long have you lived here, Merv?

MERV. I moved in almost two years ago, but with some different people. That actually was a better situation for me.

JENNIFER. Better how?

MERV. They were just a little more easy going. And I didn't end up shooting anybody, so that was better.

JENNIFER. Then you regret what happened here, today.

MERV. Regret? I don't know. On the one hand you want to say, of course I regret it, people should not fucking shoot each other! Shooting each other is what kind of solution?

JENNIFER. Merv –

MERV. It's just fucking bullshit, I know that –

JENNIFER. Merv, there is an FCC thing, about language –

MERV. *(turning back to* **JENNIFER***)* Sorry, Sorry.

JENNIFER. Let's go back to the details of how this tragedy came about.

MERV. How it came about? I don't know. She wanted to turn off my T.V.

JENNIFER. Is that a metaphor?

MERV. No, she really wanted to turn it off. Do you think that television makes people stupid, Jennifer? Alice here keeps insisting that it does and she is sincerely annoying, but I'm starting to think she has a point. Because I think watching television – and I watch a lot, I sit around and watch it like all the time, and I'm not like a brainiac or anything but I am not a stupid person but I'll tell you, Jennifer – you think about things like *Moby Dick*, that used to be like, popular entertainment – not popular, I think *Moby Dick* was actually a flop but that's you know, normal people, you, me, used to hang out reading interesting books and having conversation, just hanging out with someone like Benjamin Franklin and shooting the shit, that's what they did to relax.

JENNIFER. Let's talk about your parents.

MERV. My parents were really nice people this isn't their fault, although I had this older sister, don't get me started. But that's not, psychology isn't news, Jennifer! Or maybe it is. I don't know anymore. I think that frankly, television doesn't just make us stupid, it also makes us depressed. All those bright colors! And everyone looks so pretty and and real. Real, how does television do that, make people look hyper-real. It makes you just want to climb in there. But then the shows are all so depressing and moronic, you end up – if that is reality? Why not just blow your brains out.

JENNIFER. So suicide is actually something that's been in your mind?

MERV. *(overlap)* And once that thought occurs to you, that you could kill yourself, theoretically, you could kill other people, there's a lot of killing going on out there, you could get in on it, and then you go into a gun store, you can buy guns at Walmarts, if you really want to know, Jennifer, they don't cost anything!

JENNIFER. Wow.

MERV. They cost less than a Playstation Three! They cost less than...killing people, killing yourself, killing a whole bunch of people, costs nothing at all in America. Why don't you put that on television? As long as all you care about is money, why don't you talk about how cheap it is to kill people?

JENNIFER. Wow. That is fascinating, a fascinating point, Merv –

MERV. But you don't, you don't put anything, and I understand, it's a drag, to talk about death, on the other hand here you are and it's not because you love St. Louis – it's because death sells. Those guys in Mumbai, that's how you pronounce it, they didn't care about getting the word out about Kashmir! They just wanted to be on television. Because that's the equation: Violence equals T.V. time. You don't even have to have a reason anymore!

JENNIFER. Merv, let's go back to your sister.

MERV. Because every day I watch the news, and it seems so clear, to me, that night is falling on our planet. We're all of us in mortal danger, as a race, history is moving to its end. And it shakes me, to the core, to wonder, could we have stopped it? Could we, as a people, have been better? Was there a moment, when we had a chance to rise into a better version of humanity itself, when was that, how did we miss it?

JENNIFER. Wow. That is, that is really profound, Merv.

MERV. And I think that's why I watch *Our House*. Because it's so moronic. And noisy. And it blocks out you know, all this other stuff. That you don't tell us. The other stuff that's out there. That's true, and frightening, but if we looked at it, it might save us.

(He sits, silent, finally. A long pause.)

JENNIFER. *(to camera)* We're talking live to Merv Masterson, who today shot two of his roommates and is holding the third hostage in a desperate attempt to communicate with America.

(Her cellphone rings.)

Just a minute please, hello?

(WES is on the other line.)

WES. Night is falling? What the fuck is this? You know this is live, and you're letting him say this shit?

JENNIFER. *(to camera)* So sorry, technical difficulties, please bear with us.

(She turns the camera off, fast. Phones start to ring. STU picks one up.)

STU. Yeah.

WES. You're dying. Don't take this wrong, but he's killing you. It's a fucking low-speed chase. Optimism. Americans like optimism.

JENNIFER. I'm trying –

STU. *(overlap)* Yes yes yes we have her on the line. Yes. She is aware.

MERV. Who's that?

WES. *(overlap)* You're trying and failing. I love you, but if you fail at this, you will be taking me and the entire network down with you, you know that?

JENNIFER. What do you expect me to do; he's a shitty interview! He shot his roommates; who could have predicted he'd be a fucking Democrat?

MERV. Hellooo...

STU. *(to WES)* They're furious. She was supposed to get those hostages out of there.

WES. I'm serious baby, the cops are a little edgy, you got to cut to the chase.

JENNIFER. The cops are "edgy?" What does that mean?

STU. *(to WES)* They're going in. They're going in. They're going in.

JENNIFER. What did he say, the police are coming in?

VINCE. Thank you thank you –

MERV. They're not coming in. Ruby Ridge.

STU. I understand that –

WES. What did he say? Was that him, what did he say?

JENNIFER. He said Ruby Ridge.

STU. *(yelling on phone)* I UNDERSTAND THAT YES.

WES. He said that? He said Ruby Ridge?

JENNIFER. *(impatient)* Yes, he said the police are not going to come in because of Ruby Ridge. So what am I supposed to do?

STU. She has to get those hostages out of there now!

WES. Do something useful would you, please? Get me the numbers!

MERV. *(overlap)* Branch Davidians –

JENNIFER. Yes, thank you, Merv. I hear you, I don't know what you're saying. But I do take it seriously.

STU. *(on the other line)* Where are we at on this, numbers wise?

MERV. Elian Gonzales.

JENNIFER. I need you to give me a minute on this.

WES. Where ARE we Stu?

STU. *(shocked)* Forty two. We're at forty two, we're at forty two.

JENNIFER. What did he say?

WES. You're at forty two and climbing,

JENNIFER. Forty two?

WES. They're not going to cut you off, baby.

MERV. Forty two. That's awesome.

WES. This is your moment, Jen, you cannot blow it! Think outside the box. Otherwise we are all in the toilet. And by the way there is a clock.

JENNIFER. Wes, stop talking shit and just tell me what to do here!

WES. Just juice it up, babe.

(He hangs up.)

(JENNIFER *thinks.* **MERV** *watches her.)*

MERV. Is something wrong? Are like the police saying they're going to come in? Because there is no need to fall for that. They're still so paranoid about Ruby Ridge, there is no way they'd do that.

JENNIFER. Yes, thank you, Merv. I hope you're right. Because I think the things you're saying here, today, are really important and I would hate it if we got cut off.

MERV. Well, can't your boyfriend just tell them to go away?

JENNIFER. *(beat)* My boyfriend?

MERV. Oh, I'm sorry. It's all over the internet, that you're, um, dating your boss.

JENNIFER. It would be considered a breach of ethics for me to date my employer. Who, by the way, is a happily married man.

MERV. I'm sorry. I mean, of course! I mean, I'm sorry I believed all this bullshit they write about you, online. It's clearly a stupid place to get information. Not like the network news.

(aside, to **VINCE***)*

Shite mosque.

(He rolls his eyes, sort of privately, but she doesn't miss it.)

JENNIFER. All right, Merv. All right. The camera is off, so let's put our cards on the table, shall we?

MERV. Were we playing cards?

JENNIFER. You got what you wanted. You commandeered the airwaves and got all your shots in, and I let you do that. But there are a whole mess of idiots out there watching you talk about the end of the universe and it's depressing people so they're about to turn us off.

MERV. They're not going to turn us off! They'll watch anything!

JENNIFER. They will not watch anything.

MERV. You underestimate the intelligence of the audience.

JENNIFER. No one is getting poor underestimating the intelligence of the American public!

MERV. But you're the ones who are doing it! You're the ones who are dumbing us down!

JENNIFER. As you said yourself no one cares how we got here. We're here now, deal with it.

MERV. Yeah, but –

JENNIFER. There are no buts! You are one of them! You just admitted it, on T.V., you are one of the complete fucking idiots who spends his whole life sitting around watching this shit! You're not allowed to complain about it! You are it!

MERV. I thought you were it!

JENNIFER. I'm not arguing with you about this, you psychopath! I'm telling you what you need to do, now. I'm going to turn that camera on, and you are going to give me the gun. Now, you are going to give it to me, now, on the air. And it's going to be great television.

MERV. I don't think so.

JENNIFER. I think so. Because unless you give up the gun, you're not getting out of here alive. Now in spite of that charming diatribe about blowing your own brains out, you're not strictly suicidal, are you.

(beat) Speak up, Merv! I can't hear you.

(They consider each other. STU and WES pace.)

STU. How long have they had that camera off?

WES. *(diffident)* A while.

STU. And you're not…scared?

WES. Scared?

STU. That guy has a gun! Aren't you worried?

WES. Oh, worried. Yeah of course I'm worried. I worry about everything, Christ, you know that. This is massive, it's a massive story about you know this event in the midwest and I just think Midwesterners go for a little more cleavage. We never got the bra with the pumps. And that nose.

STU. WES, YOU'RE OUT OF YOUR FUCKING MIND!

WES. I am not out of my mind. I know what you're saying. You're saying, Wes: You could lose. What if you lose the thing you love. But I don't think about that. And so I don't lose it. You, you think about it all the time, and you lose it all the time. The news. You go on and on and on about the news. But you've already lost it! No one cares about it! And I'm here – I'm your friend, Stu. And I'm saying Stu: You could win. You could win the news back. You could win. Look, the feed's back on!

(JENNIFER in a spot.)

JENNIFER. Thank you for your patience. Thank you, ladies and gentlemen. I am here with Merv Masterson, who earlier today opened fire on two of his housemates during a routine house meeting which sadly went awry. Since then, Mr. Masterson has refused to release the victims of his crime, and they remain where they fell in this blood-soaked saga.

(to MERV)

Mr. Masterson – Merv- you know that this house is surrounded by police officers, and that they grow increasingly impatient, waiting for you to release your hostages.

MERV. I won't do it.

JENNIFER. At any moment they could attempt to take the house.

MERV. Well, I don't advise that they do that! Because I have a gun here, and if anyone tries to attack, I'm gonna kill everybody! Including Jennifer Ramirez.

(He holds up his weapon and puts it to her head. She freezes a little bit.)

I'm doing it for you, America!

JENNIFER. *(sitting very still)* You're angry, aren't you, Merv.

MERV. Gee, you think?

JENNIFER. And you're in pain. And that's why you're lashing out, isn't it?

MERV. Yes.

JENNIFER. Merv – I really want to hear about everything that is troubling you. We all do. But first, you have to give me the gun.

MERV. No!

JENNIFER. Please Merv. Give me the gun.

MERV. I'm afraid.

JENNIFER. Don't be afraid, Merv. People care about you. We all want to help you. But you have to give me the gun.

(She is very gentle. He reaches out slowly and gives her the gun.)

WES. Awesome.

(JENNIFER has the gun. She turns it around in her hand. Then, cold blooded, she shoots him. All yell.)

STU. Whoa! She shot him!

WES. *(overlap)* Yes! Yes! Yes!

MERV. *(stunned, overlap)* I'm shot! You shot me!

JENNIFER. *(to camera)* I'm fine. Everybody. I'm fine.

MERV. Ow. It hurts. You know, it really – hurts!

JENNIFER. You're fine, Merv.

(to camera, serious)

It's just a shoulder wound, he's going to be all right!

MERV. Easy for you to say. You shot me!

JENNIFER. I did what I felt I had to. To secure the safety of everyone here.

(*then looking around*)

I think we all need a little privacy. Please.

(*She turns the camera off.*)

(WES *goes to join* **JENNIFER.**)

WES. That was genius.

JENNIFER. Thanks, Wes.

(WES *turns to* STU.)

WES. You don't want to be a part of this?

STU. No. I don't. I quit.

WES. I said it from the start: You're an artist. And I mean that in the most profound sense of the word, beyond art itself, art, who gives a shit about art, art is over! But what you did. What this is. Drama. News. Television. You are giving birth to a whole new consciousness. Reality fusing and re creating itself in whole new patterns, time, space, knowledge, truth, all is redefined in moments like this. Reality. America. We will ask ourselves forever after this moment, how it changed. And I know – and you know – we will always know: It was you.

JENNIFER. And the numbers?

WES. Through the roof. Through the fucking roof.

(*He kisses her.*)

Go on, baby. You're a star. (*then*) Sell the gun a little, honey.

JENNIFER. I'm on it.

(JENNIFER *takes the gun, smiles at him and goes out of the house. As the door opens, all hell breaks loose: lights, cameras, shouting reporters. The door shuts behind her.*)

WES. Hey.

MERV. Hey.

WES. I'm –

MERV. I know who you are.

WES. How is that?

MERV. It hurts. *(beat)* So where are the fucking cops?

WES. I asked them to give us a minute. *(beat)* You watch a
   lot of television?

MERV. Why?

WES. Look, I can get them in here, if you're in a hurry.

MERV. No, no. I...I do, I watch television. And I'm not
   apologizing for that.

WES. Am I asking you to?

MERV. I just mean, you know, some people act like television is stupid, and...

WES. Who acts like that?

MERV. Everybody.

WES. No, nobody says that. Intellectual shitheads, maybe.

MERV. No, everybody.

WES. Nobody says it to me.

VINCE. Television is stupid.

WES. Who are you, what are you doing here? Can't you
   make yourself useful? Get some help for these girls
   before they bleed to death? For god's sake!

GRIGSBY. She's gone.

WES. What?

VINCE. She's dead. She bled to death.

GRIGSBY. *(accusing)* She bled to death, Merv!

WES. Yeah, yeah, you're right, that's bad. But you're alive!
   Come on. This girl needs treatment. Go let the cops
   know things are under control, would you?

VINCE. Come on, Grigsby.

   *(He picks her up, carries her out the door. There is
   another moment of silence. Then –)*

WES. She wasn't supposed to shoot you, was she?

MERV. She...

WES. Don't lie to me. You two, you cooked the story, while
   the camera was off. It's fine. It's reality, you know, reality T.V., it's cooked.

MERV. Yeah, we cooked it.

WES. But not all of it. The surprise on your face. I was surprised too, she's fabulous, there is no one like her, but who knew she had that in her.

MERV. Yeah, she rocked it.

WES. She did.

MERV. Well...for me it kinda wasn't so great.

WES. What a show! And you. You're very – I like you, Merv.

MERV. Oh, good.

WES. A lot of people might look at you and think sociopath but I see the kind of genius that only television can create. I think there might be something we could do together.

MERV. Really. I mean I might be going to jail.

WES. Oh no no.

MERV. I think I am.

WES. Come on, because of this?

MERV. Well. Yes.

WES. Post-O.J.-television and the law leave a lot of room for improvisation. I mean the trial will be riveting, and it could be a very close call, but that doesn't necessarily mean jail time.

MERV. I did like being on T.V. but I don't know.

WES. You trying to negotiate? Because this isn't a negotiation. I mean, you are not going to hold me up for a share of the internet download here. Those fucking writers, I'd like to hang every fucking one of them fucking piece-of-shit writers thinking what? What do they think? They think America CARES about WRITERS? I could pick some prostitute up off the street, she'd be a better writer than anybody in the WGA. On either fucking coast although in New York you know they at least read the occasional book. They can't write one but they know how to read! You know how to read?

MERV. Yeah.

WES. You don't have to. It's okay. Just don't go expecting a piece of the internet.

MERV. I won't.

WES. Good. We'll talk. Just one rule: You cannot ever say anything mean about Jennifer. I'll fucking fire you, if you do.

MERV. I wouldn't. I love her.

WES. Me too, kid. Me too.

(He leaves. **MERV** *is alone on the stage for a moment. He looks around. Fade out.)*

End of Play

OTHER TITLES AVAILABLE FROM SAMUEL FRENCH

MAURITIUS

Theresa Rebeck

Comedy / 3m, 2f / Interior

Stamp collecting is far more risky than you think. After their mother's death, two estranged half-sisters discover a book of rare stamps that may include the crown jewel for collectors. One sister tries to collect on the windfall, while the other resists for sentimental reasons. In this gripping tale, a seemingly simple sale becomes dangerous when three seedy, high-stakes collectors enter the sisters' world, willing to do anything to claim the rare find as their own.

"Unsurprisingly for a writer with extensive experience in TV police procedurals like "*NYPD Blue*" and "*Law & Order: Criminal Intent,*" one of Rebeck's strengths is her skill at stitching tension into every exchange. The five characters in *Mauritius* pair up and face off in shifting configurations, the emotionally fraught edges of their twisty encounters made all the more intriguing by the fact that items as apparently innocuous as postage stamps fuel the friction."
– *Variety*

"One wouldn't think that the subject of rare stamps would make for gripping, entertaining theater, but Theresa Rebeck's *Mauritius*, being given its Broadway premiere by the Manhattan Theatre Club, proves otherwise...The sort of well-made, engrossing and unpretentious play rarely encountered on Broadway these days, *Mauritius* is a welcome introduction to the fall season."
– *The Hollywood Reporter*

OTHER TITLES AVAILABLE FROM SAMUEL FRENCH

THE SCENE

Theresa Rebeck

Drama / 2m, 2f

A young social climber leads an actor into an extra-marital affair, from which he then creates a full-on downward spiral into alcoholism and bummery. His wife runs off with his best friend, his girlfriend leaves, and he's left with … nothing.

"Ms. Rebeck's dark-hued morality tale contains enough fresh insights into the cultural landscape to freshen what is essentially a classic boy-meets-bad-girl story...Ms. Rebeck is an established playwright who has also worked in television, and she clearly knows how the savage, mercurial economics of the entertainment industry can shatter the fragile ego and wreak havoc on domestic equilibrium."
– *The New York Times*

"Rebeck's wickedly scathing observations about the sort of self-obsessed New Yorkers who pursue their own interests at the cost of their morality and loyalty."
– *New York Post*

"*The Scene* is utterly delightful in its comedic performances, and its slowly unraveling plot is thought-provoking and gut-wrenching."
– *Show Business Weekly*

"On the surface, it may appear to be just a bubbly boulevard comedy. And, on the surface, that's what Theresa Rebeck's *The Scene* uproariously is. But underneath lurks something much darker, almost tragic. That is how great, double-bottomed comedies are: Think *The Misanthrope*, think *Who's Afraid of Virginia Woolf?*...Finally, though, it is the writing that triumphs in the all- important details. There are frantic sentence fragments, stammering reiterations, dragged-out burbles, and every current noncommunicative cliche sovereignly ridiculed. And let us not overlook Rebeck's ability to put sex onstage: erotically, farcically, and with clinical dissection. Laugh your way into this one."
– *Bloomberg.com*